W9-CDD-322

Copyright © 2012 by Disney Enterprises, Inc. All rights reserved. Published by Disney Press, an
imprint of Disney Book Group. No part of this book may be reproduced or transmitted in any
form or by any means, electronic or mechanical, including photocopying, recording, or by any
information storage and retrieval system, without written permission from the publisher.
For information address Disney Press, 114 Fifth Avenue, New York, New York 10011-5690.

First Edition
10 9 8 7 6 5 4 3 2 1
ISBN 978-1-4231-8407-2
F322-8368-0-12313
Printed in the USA

Sofia
the First

Written by
Catherine Hapka

Illustrated by
Grace Lee

Disney PRESS

New York

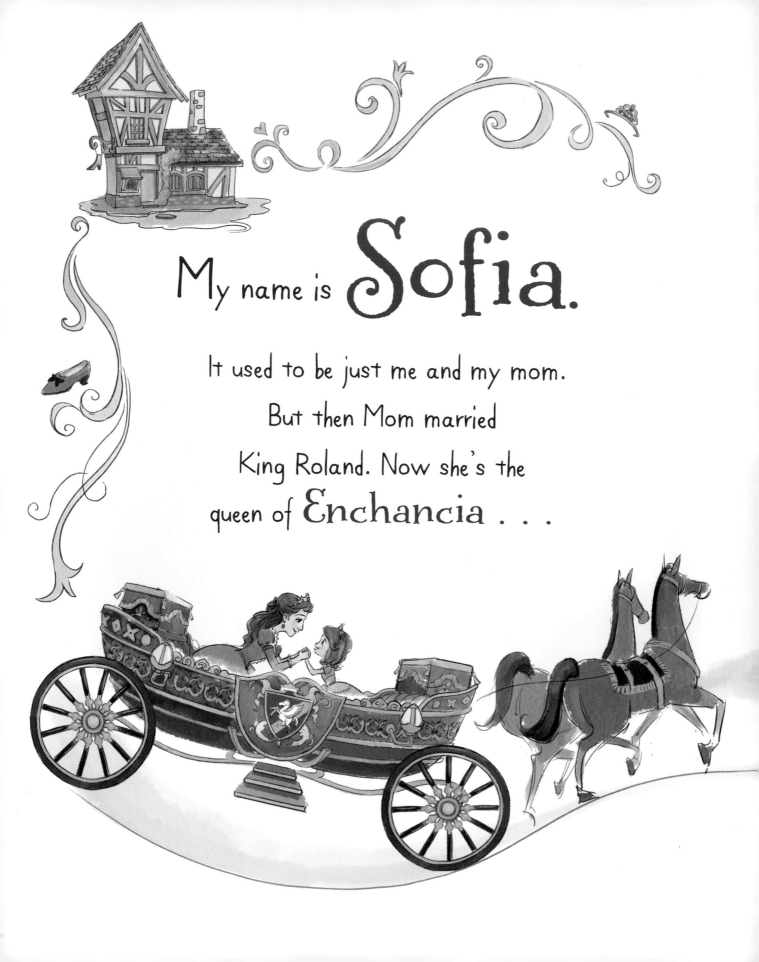

My name is Sofia.

It used to be just me and my mom.
But then Mom married
King Roland. Now she's the
queen of Enchancia . . .

and I'm a
princess.

The trouble is, I don't really know anything about being a **princess.**

I never had to do a
royal wave . . .

I'm not sure when
to curtsy . . .

or even which fork
to use at dinner.

I'll never be as perfect a
princess as my
new stepsister, Amber.

"Just be yourself and you'll be fine,"
Mom tells me.

I'm not sure that will work. How can I be **myself** and be a princess at the same time?

Then King Roland—um,
I mean my new dad—tries to help.
He gives me a beautiful necklace
called the

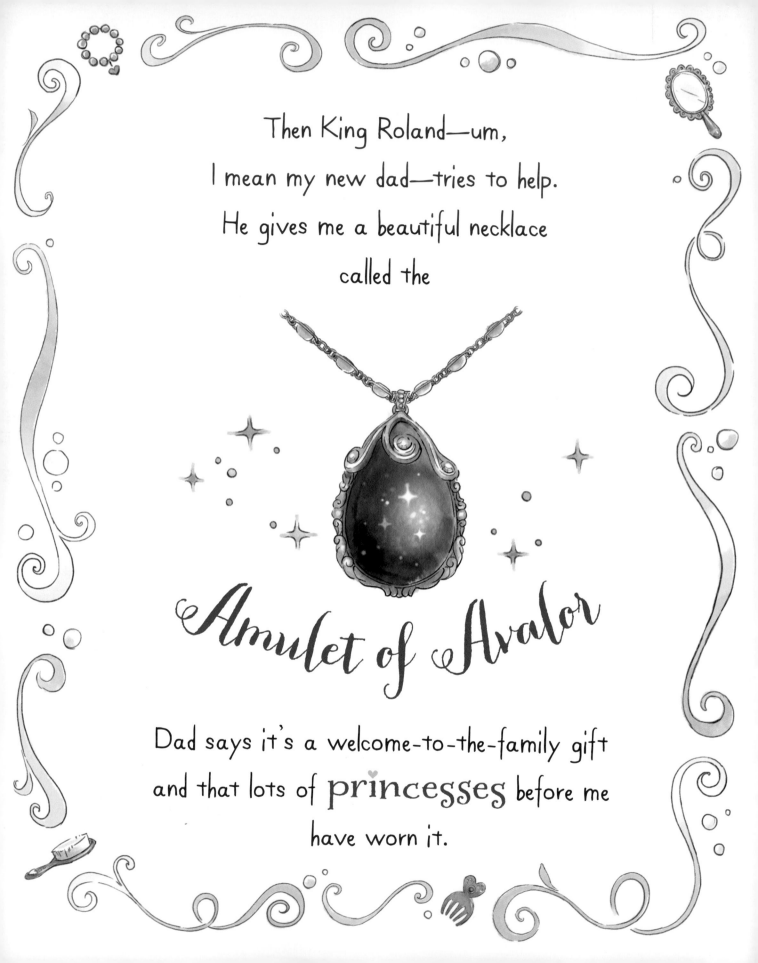

Amulet of Avalor

Dad says it's a welcome-to-the-family gift
and that lots of princesses before me
have worn it.

Then he tells me we're having a royal ball in my honor. He says we'll dance the first waltz together. That's another thing I don't know how to do—dance!

Maybe there will be a dance class at my new school, Royal Prep Academy. The headmistresses are three fairies named

Flora,

Fauna, and

Merryweather.

They promise to
teach me everything
about being a
princess.

Hooray! I do have a dance class! Amber lends me a
pair of special shoes. I think she's starting to like me.

Oh, no!

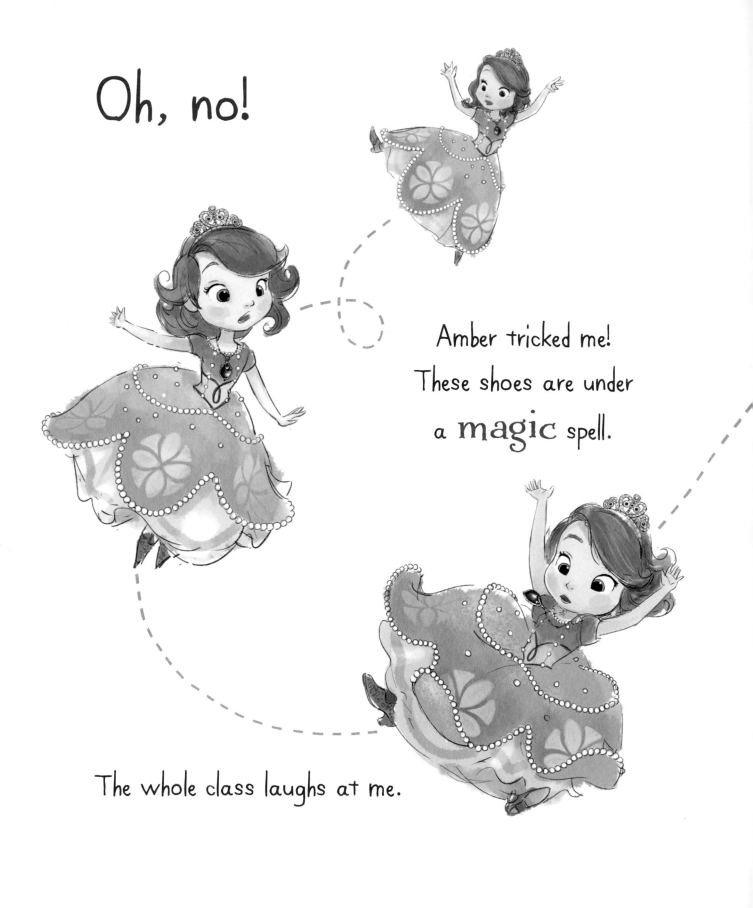

Amber tricked me!
These shoes are under
a **magic** spell.

The whole class laughs at me.

But even worse,
I still don't know
how to waltz,
and

the

ball

is

tonight!

Then I remember Cedric, the sorcerer at the castle. James, my stepbrother, says he has all sorts of **magic** spells.

I ask Cedric to help. He writes down some **magic** words. He says if I recite them at the ball, I'll be able to waltz like a real **princess.**

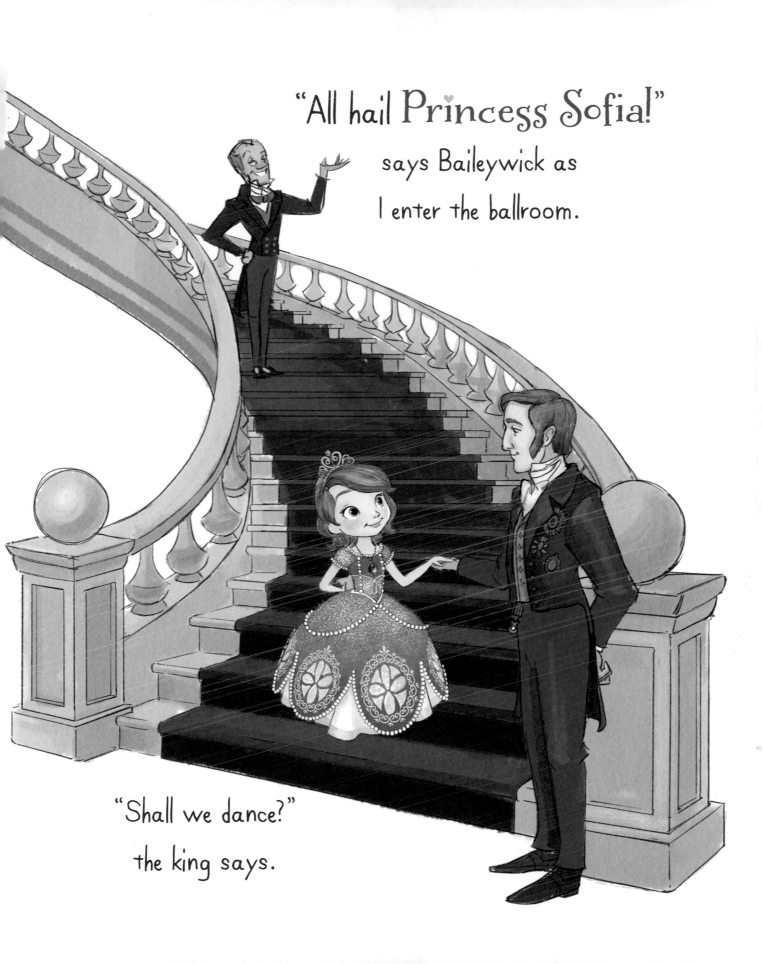

"All hail Princess Sofia!" says Baileywick as I enter the ballroom.

"Shall we dance?" the king says.

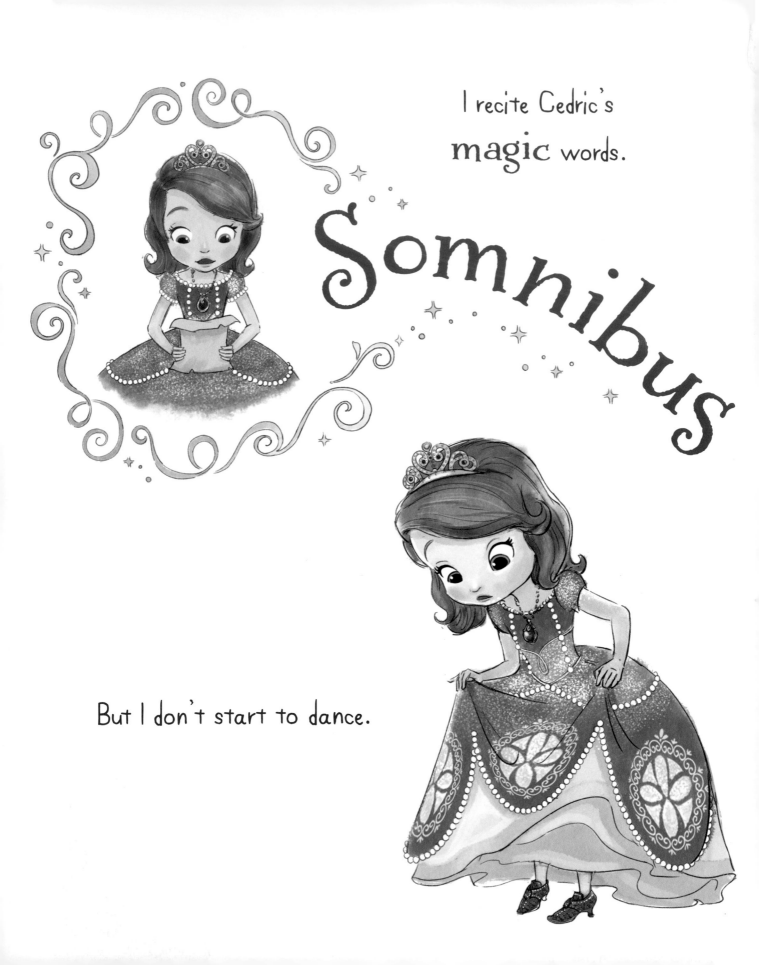

I recite Cedric's **magic** words.

Somnibus

But I don't start to dance.

Populis Cella!

Instead, everyone at the ball falls asleep— even Cedric!

Oh, no!

What have I done? "Help!" I cry.

Suddenly,

my amulet

glows

and

Cinderella appears!

"Your amulet brought me here," she tells me. "When a **princess** is in trouble, another will come to help."

"Can you reverse the spell, Cinderella?"
"No, I can't, but your new sister might be able to help."

"But Amber's been so mean to me!" I say.

Cinderella knows what it's like to
have mean stepsisters.
"I wish I had given my stepsisters
a second chance," she says.
"Perhaps that's what Amber needs."

Then she **disappears**.

Amber is still in her room. She never
made it to the ball. She finally tells me
why she's been acting so mean.

"I was worried that everyone would like
you more than me," she says sadly.

"No one could ever be as perfect a
princess as you, Amber!"

I tell her about Cedric's **magic** spell. We search his workshop,

and find a spell that will wake everyone up.

We hurry to the ballroom.

"Wait," Amber says. "I owe you a dance lesson."

Now I know we're true sisters—and **ever-after friends.**

When I get to the ballroom, I say the
magic words, and everyone wakes up.
Then the king and I begin to waltz.

I look over at Amber and smile.
I can't believe how happy I am. . . .
I think I'm going to fit into this
royal family after all.

"Sofia," my dad says, "I'm so proud of you.
You dance wonderfully!"
"Thank you, Your Majesty—I mean, Dad."
"You know, Sofia, being a princess is about
having a good heart. And you're going to make
a great princess."

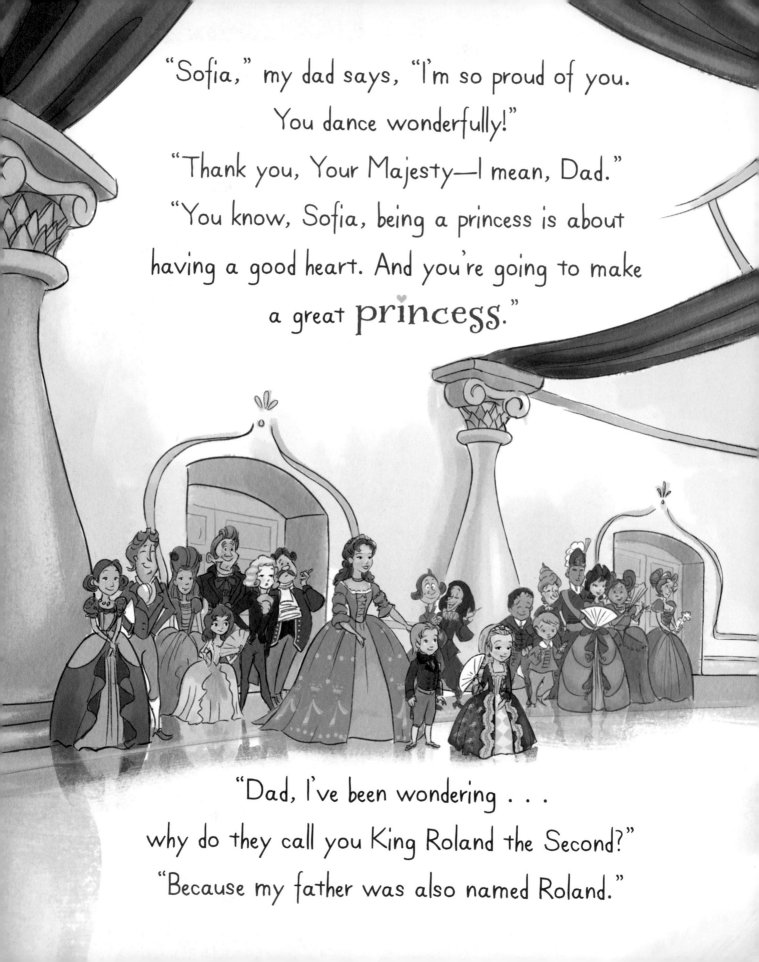

"Dad, I've been wondering . . .
why do they call you King Roland the Second?"
"Because my father was also named Roland."

"Well . . ." I say, "I guess that makes me

Sofia the First!"

And I am one princess who can't wait to see
what happens tomorrow and all the days
happily ever after!

The End